Molly's Christmas Miracle

Cheryl Wright

Copyright

Molly's Christmas Miracle

Copyright ©2020

by Cheryl Wright

Cover Artist: Black Widow Books

Dedication

To Margaret Tanner, my very dear friend and fellow author, for her enduring encouragement and friendship.

To Alan, my husband of over forty-six years, who has been a relentless supporter of my writing and dreams for many years.

To Virginia McKevitt, cover artist and friend, who always creates the most amazing covers for my books.

To You, my wonderful readers, who encourage me to continue writing these stories. It is such a joy knowing so many of you enjoy reading my stories as much as I love writing them for you.

Table of Contents

Chapter One

Fool's Chance, Montana - 1880

Molly Mason was fed up.

She was sick of being passed over by men folk in Fool's Chance. Sick of not being asked to the dance, and over being one of the few spinsters left in town.

Could she help it if she had to work long hours? Or if she was the best seamstress for miles around?

As much as that sounded vain, Molly knew it was true.

She did her job more than well, and people came from outlying towns to use her services. When she'd inherited the store from her aunt, she was already an accomplished seamstress. Aunt Rose sent for her when Molly's mother had died and she was the impressionable age of eleven.

The day she arrived in Fool's Chance, her education began.

Aunt Rose insisted she attend school, she wouldn't have it any other way. But after school, Molly was in the store, soaking in as much as her young mind would absorb.

Back then, the town was much busier. With the promise of gold to be found, families flocked to the tiny town of Fool's Chance. As the name implied, they were Fool's Chance – of finding their own pot of gold.

Very few did. But they'd been here so long they decided to call the place home. The womenfolk, fed up with living in tents, insisted their husbands build houses for them.

Aunt Rose knew an opportunity when she saw it, and opened up her little store. Making custom gowns for the ladies of Fool's Chance quickly became her livelihood. And she thrived on it.

Her husband had passed on some years earlier, and Aunt Rose was struggling to survive. She'd always made her own clothes, and decided that was the path she would take.

Molly adored working at the shop. Loved the smell and the feel of the fabrics. Sometimes she would brush her cheek against them, especially if she was feeling low.

Aunt Rose's pride and joy, her sewing machine, sat in the back of the store. Her uncle gifted it to her when she'd opened the store. He owned a clothing factory in the city back then, and this particular machine was at the end of its factory life. He figured if she got even a few years from it, Rose would be happy. Many years later it was still going strong. Countless beautiful gowns had been created on that little cast-off sewing machine.

Molly glanced up as the little bell over the door tinkled. Miss Hadie Winsome from nearby Ellisdale smiled at her. "Time for a new gown, Molly," she said, heading for the most expensive rolls of fabric in the store.

As much as she knew her state of spinsterhood wouldn't go away any time soon, the distraction was a welcomed relief.

* * *

Molly had a mouthful of pins.

This was a first fitting for her repeat customer. She glanced at Hadie and sighed. "Please stand still, Miss Winsome. This needs to be accurate."

Every year without fail, she arrived to be fitted for a new ball gown. Molly was sure Hadie saw herself as the belle of the ball. The Christmas Gala ball that was.

Fool's Chance had never held a ball to her knowledge, and she wondered if it wouldn't be fun to have one. Perhaps next year? It was surely too late this year to be organizing an event such as this.

Besides, where would it be held?

The Fool's Chance church hall wasn't very large, but then again, the township didn't have a lot of citizens.

She sighed again. Wishful thinking, especially coming from a spinster such as herself. But then again, Hadie was a spinster too. Perhaps she was hoping to pick up a husband at the ball?

"Is it fun," she asked out of the blue, already wanting to take her words back. What her customers did was none of her business.

"Is what fun, Molly?" the other woman asked, totally perplexed. Then realization dawned. "Oh, the ball do you mean?"

Molly nodded, her mouth once again full of pins. "It's magical," Hadie said dreamily. "It's always decorated for Christmas, with colorful decorations everywhere, giving it a real Christmas feel. The floor of the ballroom is always highly polished, making it easy to glide along the floor with gentlemen who are looking for a wife."

"It sounds wonderful." Molly glanced at the woman standing next to her. "I wish we could hold a ball here in Fool's Chance," she said, knowing it would never happen.

"Pffft," Hadie said, waving her hand about. "Fool's Chance is far too small to hold a ball. It takes a lot of effort. Besides, where would you have it?"

It was as though she'd read Molly's thoughts. "I wondered the same myself," Molly said, then went back to pinning the waistband of Hadie's ballgown.

The little bell over the door tinkled, and Molly put her head around the doorway of the fitting room. "I won't be a moment," she called out.

"That's fine. We can wait."

Molly startled at the masculine voice. It was rare to have men enter her domain. In fact, this was probably a first. Generally the men left their wives at the door, arranging to come back when they were done.

She carefully helped Hadie out of the gown, ensuring all the pins stayed in place. She glanced at her diary. "Same time Friday," she asked her favorite customer.

Hadie nodded and was added to the diary. Molly was meticulous about her bookings. It would never do to overbook – each customer deserved their own special time.

She helped the other woman into her thick coat and handed the reticule to her, then walked her to the front door. Acknowledging her new customers on her way.

"Thank you, Molly. You're a miracle worker," Hadie said, giving her a quick hug, and then she was gone.

"I'm so sorry for keeping you," Molly told the newcomers. "I'm Molly Mason, and I'm the owner and seamstress of this store."

The young gent reached out and shook her hand. She felt warmth at his touch despite the cold weather. "I'm very pleased to meet you," he said, sounding like he meant it. "I'm Daniel Emerson, and this is my sister Eloise." He indicated the young woman standing next to him, and she did a little curtsy.

"I'm very pleased to meet you both," Molly said, wrenching her hand back. She wriggled her fingers, endeavoring to stop the current surging through them.

"My sister requires a ball gown. We were told you're the best, and so here we are." He straightened his shoulders and stood tall, no doubt waiting for her to respond.

She watched as Eloise glanced about the store, studying the various materials. Her eyes fell on a roll of velvet in the deepest of purple.

Molly screwed up her face.

"You don't like that one?" Mr Emerson asked.

Molly checked herself. She must stop doing that – Aunt Rose was forever griping when she did it. Especially when customers were around.

"I'm sorry, I didn't mean to be rude." She walked over to a roll of cobalt blue silk. "This one," she said confidently. "It will bring out the color in your sister's blue eyes."

Eloise reached out and touched it. "It's soft and pretty. I like it." She smiled for the first time since entering the store.

Mr Emerson grinned at her. "You know your stuff."

It was a statement, not a question, but Molly answered anyway. "Of course I do, Mr Emerson," she said a little huffy. "I trained for many years to do this work. I listen to the requests of my customers, but try to guide them to fabrics that will compliment them."

"Daniel, please." Eloise looked exasperated at her brother's comments.

He turned to Eloise. "Are you happy? Do you wish to go ahead?"

She nodded. "Can I book in for a fitting?"

She asked the question so softly, Molly almost missed it, but snatched up her bookings diary. "Are you in Fool's Chance long?" she asked. "I can do a fitting Monday next week at 10am if that works. Otherwise it will be another week I'm afraid."

Eloise's face dropped. "But I need it for the Christmas Gala." She turned to her brother. "What am I going to do?" Tears began to well in her eyes, and Molly felt bad.

It was always busy at this time of the year. The young women hoping to find themselves a husband left it to the last minute. Every year without fail.

"I'm really sorry," Molly said, genuinely upset for Eloise. "It's always like this in November. It's the Christmas Gala," she added, trying to explain.

"Thanks anyway." Daniel Emerson sounded deflated, and turned to leave, guiding his sister toward the door. He suddenly stopped. "Would it help if I paid you a bonus?"

Molly stared at him. Didn't he realize it was a matter of time, not money?

"The thing is, we lost our parents in a stagecoach accident recently, and this was meant to cheer my sister up."

Molly swallowed down the emotion that hit her in the gut. She knew what that felt like.

"We've only recently found out about the ball." He was asking for something totally unselfish, something to take away his sister's sadness.

He turned away, the sorrow evident on his face.

"Wait!" Molly called to his back before her brain kicked in. Her heart beat rapidly. She had no idea how she would pull this off, but she had to find a way. "Can you come back tomorrow morning at seven? I'll try to work something out."

He stared at her momentarily, then grinned. "Really? My goodness, you are terrific. Thank you on behalf of my dear sister." Daniel stepped forward and gave her a gentle hug.

It startled her, but she liked the feel of his arms around her.

"My goodness," he said, sounding shocked. "I do apologise. I'm just a little overwhelmed and quite excited. Thank you," he said, taking her hands, which were dwarfed by his. "We'll see you tomorrow." He exited the shop, and tipped his hat to her as she watched him through the front window.

What on earth had she gotten herself into?

Chapter Two

Molly stared at her booking diary. She wasn't sure how she would pull this off.

She normally started at eight, and allocated the first hour of the day to tidying and cleaning her work room.

That was, unless there was a pressing booking.

There were always threads on the floor and bits of material everywhere. It was an endless task, but Aunt Rose had taught her early on to ignore the mess, and continue on. If she sacrificed her clean up time, she would be able to fit Eloise in.

Besides, much of that hour was her down time where she had a coffee and prepared herself for the busy day ahead.

Instead of closing up shop, Molly picked up the broom and began to sweep. She would clean now, and not have to worry in the morning.

She nodded her head. That was a much better idea. That way she could devote a whole hour to finding out what Eloise wanted, and deciding on a design for her. The material was already chosen – unless her new customer changed her mind.

Molly snatched up the broom and shovel and swept the loose threads into the rubbish. She dusted around her sewing machine, then went into the main part of the shop, dusting around the rolls of materials.

Aunt Rose was always insistent they bought the best materials. Customers who attended this store knew they were buying the best quality, and deserved it.

The cobalt blue silk she'd suggested for Eloise was one of the most expensive in the store. She already had a design in mind – one that would highlight the young woman's best features.

She picked up her sketch pad and pencil and began to sketch out a design. With wide shoulders, and a high cut neckline, she was sure Mr Emerson would approve. The bodice would taper down to accentuate the waistline, but wouldn't be too cozy. She was sure he wouldn't approve of that.

Below the waist the dress would fan out into an A-line style.

She sat back and stared at her sketch. Her heart skipped a beat. This would be one of her best designs, she was sure of it.

Molly pulled down the carved wooden box left to her by her mother. It was where she kept all her ribbons and embellishments for her creations.

There would surely be something here to accentuate the gown she'd just created. It needed to be simple and elegant, but couldn't overtake the gown itself.

Eloise Emerson was a beautiful young woman, and this gown needed to suit her perfectly.

Molly set up her workstation ready for the seven a.m. meeting, then blew out the lantern. The moonlight filtering through the front window was always enough for her to see her way out.

She locked the front door, and stared at her window dressing. The dresses displayed there were made by her dear Aunt Rose.

She could have changed them, there was no doubt, but Molly left them there to remind herself of her roots.

Without her precious aunt, Molly wouldn't be doing the thing she loved best.

Her eyes skimmed the window until they found the name painted across the glass. *A Stitch in Time*. Aunt Rose sure had a way with words.

The name suited the business perfectly. A faint smile came to her face remembering her dear aunt and the first day she arrived into her care.

They were virtual strangers. Molly had already been shoved from one relative to another, until Aunt Rose put a stop to it.

Her aunt closed up the shop for a whole week, and collected her. She had enough clothing to get her through the return trip, but that was all. Aunt Rose vowed to make Molly a whole new wardrobe, and she did.

She began work almost the moment they arrived back in Fool's Chance.

Molly reached out and traced the words with her fingers. Her eyes welled with the memories, and she brushed at her eyes, trying to force the tears back.

She occasionally had supper at the diner, but she wouldn't tonight. She didn't feel like much anyway.

Molly made her way to the middle of town, and the wishing well. It was said to have magical powers, but she knew that was just a fallacy.

It did however, seem to have some pull on her. When she was feeling low, Molly would make her way to the wishing well and sit on the side of it, careful to hold on tight in case she slipped backwards.

No one would ever know she was there, and she would be gone forever.

She slowly walked toward the well, lifting her skirts to stop the sleet dirtying the edges. December would be here soon enough, and the snow would settle in.

At least they had another few weeks before that happened. When the snow arrived, the cold would really set in.

Then the fireplace in the fitting room would be burning at full steam. It got quite cold back there otherwise.

Molly arrived at the wishing well and sat on its edge. She contemplated her life, wondering if she would be a spinster forever.

She shook herself – she couldn't afford to think that way. She looked to the sky and glanced at the moon. Tonight was as full moon, and Molly always found herself reminiscing when the moon was full.

She wasn't sure what caused it, but it seemed to always have that affect on her. She turned and looked down into the water. The reflection of the moon drew her in, she couldn't look away.

A sound behind her startled Molly, and she quickly stood, falling backwards as she did, until two strong hands grabbed her and halted her greatest fear - tumbling into the well.

Her heart beat rapidly, and she put her hands to her chest. She could have easily fall in. She could have drowned.

She stood dazed. "Are you alright, Miss Mason?" She glanced up to see Daniel Emerson standing in front of her. He looked rather concerned.

For her. For her safety.

"I, I, I'm a bit stunned, is all."

His hands fell to his sides, but she could still feel the heat where they'd held her.

"Take deep breaths," he said, leading her over to a bench seat. "You're probably in shock."

She nodded.

"I'm really sorry," he continued. "I didn't mean to startle you. My sister fell asleep, so I decided to take a stroll around town."

"I was heading home to make supper." She began to stand.

He stood with her. "Allow me to buy you supper at the diner."

"I, I couldn't. Besides I have eggs and bread at home – it's all planned."

He stared at her. "Eggs and bread? That is no supper for a lady who works as hard as you do. I insist on buying your supper."

She shook her head. "I can't. It's not right." And it wasn't. This was a man she'd only met today.

His eyes looked pained. "Perhaps look at it as a thank you for helping my sister."

She stared at him, astounded by his kind gesture. "I guess that would be alright." She was still pensive, but she was hungry, and supper at the diner sounded much more palatable than scrambled eggs.

Daniel Emerson grinned at her, then guided her toward the diner.

* * *

Molly arrived at *A Stitch in Time* early. It wouldn't do to have her customers waiting on the doorstep for her.

What would people think? What would Daniel think? Especially after he'd treated her like a queen last night.

She was sure she wouldn't get through the huge meal placed in front of her, but with Daniel's encouragement she did.

And she felt better for it.

She grinned. She'd had supper with a very nice gentleman. That stopped Molly in her tracks. It had been a first – she'd never been invited to supper before. Not by a man anyway.

She felt her cheeks heat up, then shook herself. It wasn't as though they'd been on a date. Daniel had made it clear the invitation was a thank you for accommodating his sister at the last minute.

Off the fitting room, right down the back of the shop, was another room. It was similar to a kitchen, only tiny. Aunt Rose had realized long ago a small wood stove would be to their advantage. The fire was always burning, even in the summer, and a kettle full of water always on the boil. Sewing was thirsty work, she always said. Molly smiled at the memory.

There were two small cupboards with locks, and they'd always been for the women to place their personal items. You never knew who would come into the store.

Molly put her reticule in the small cupboard, as well as her sandwich and apple for lunch.

She'd just finished securing the lock when she heard the tinkle of the bell.

"Good morning," she heard Daniel call out.

She rushed into the main part of the store, anxious to show Eloise her sketch. "Good morning," she said excitedly.

"I enjoyed supper last night," Daniel said.

She smiled at him, but Eloise didn't seem impressed. "You had supper together? Why didn't I know about this?"

Daniel turned to her and frowned. "You were asleep, and I was hungry. I bumped into Molly at the wishing well."

"I, I'm sorry, Miss Emerson," Molly began. "It won't happen again."

Daniel intervened quickly. "I hope it does, and it has nothing to do with my sister, or our transaction." He made it perfectly clear what he thought of his sister's interference, and it sent warmth down Molly's spine.

He turned to smile at her. "We don't want to hold you up, Molly."

"You're on first-name terms?" Eloise did not seem at all happy, but Molly decided to ignore her comment. Besides, Daniel was right – it was none of his sister's business.

Eloise glared at him, but Daniel chose to ignore her, instead focusing on Molly. "What do you have there," he asked, indicating the sketch pad in her hands.

"After you left last night, I had an idea." She lifted the sketch pad to show them.

Daniel grinned, and his sister's eyes opened wide. Her hands went to her heart. "Oh my goodness, that is stunning!" she said, making Molly's heartbeat quicken.

"If you're happy with this design, we can start right now." She ushered Eloise into the fitting room, leaving Daniel standing in the store. "Come back in an hour," she told him, then turned to her customer.

"First I'll need to get some measurements. Then you'll need to make some decisions – about fabric, ribbons etc."

Eloise nodded, but barely said a word. Molly wondered if Eloise was still cross at her for dining with her brother.

The hour seemed to go quickly, and Daniel came back on time as requested. Molly handed him an account for the gown, deposit and payment plan laid out clearly.

He seemed taken aback by it, and she worried it was too much. Her heartbeat quickened waiting for him to speak.

"This is terrible, Molly," he said, and she immediately felt ill. Had he changed his mind? She couldn't make it any cheaper, it wouldn't be worth her while. "You need to ask for full payment upfront. What if you did all that work, and the customer pulled out at the last minute?"

She stared at him. What did he mean? It's the way Aunt Rose worked, and she followed suit.

"You are in business. People are used to paying before the product is provided." He reached into his pocket and pulled out a hand carved leather wallet.

Her eyes opened wide at the wad of notes she saw there. He counted out the full amount stated on the account, then added an additional forty dollars.

She handed the excess back to him. "I can't take that," she said quietly. "But thank you."

He frowned. "You can, and you will. You are arriving early to work to accommodate my sister, and you will be paid for it. Take it as a bonus, as we first discussed."

She bit on her bottom lip. What should she do?

"You must take it. *Please.*"

Eloise stepped forward. "You must Molly. I know the gown will be beautiful. Besides, Daniel can afford it." She grinned and he frowned at her.

He pulled out his pocket watch. "We must leave. Molly has another customer arriving shortly. When do you want to see Eloise again?"

"How long are you in Fool's Chance? I can make it the same time tomorrow if you're still around."

"We will be here as long as it takes. Arrangements can be fluid." He tipped his hat and guided his sister toward the door.

Molly looked down at the wad of money in her hand. She would have to run to the Mercantile and deposit it in the bank before her next customer arrived. She didn't want to risk having such a large amount of money in the store – even locked in the cupboard out back.

Chapter Three

Molly was locking up when she heard a sound behind her and startled.

"It's just me, Daniel."

She turned, and the moonlight played across his face. It was a nice face, with his shiny brown eyes and wavy brown hair to match, and his clean shaven jaw.

He was always dressed impeccably – she hadn't seen him in anything but tailored suits. Her eyes slid downwards at his leather shoes peaking out below the hem of his trousers. When she looked up again he was grinning.

She'd been caught. Molly knew she was blushing; the heat in her cheeks told her so. Thank goodness he couldn't see it in the moonlight.

He leaned forward and brushed her cheeks with his fingers. "You look cute when you blush." She was so wrong, and felt the heat deepen even more.

At that moment, she wanted the ground to open up and swallow her.

"It's alright, Molly. I don't mind." He pulled his hand away, and she felt hollow. When did a man's touch light up her whole being?

This was a first for her. Molly had always been far too busy to have anything to do with men. Not that anyone had ever been interested.

"You look lovely, by the way." He offered his arm and she hooked hers through it. "I booked a table for two at the diner. I hope you don't mind."

She stared at him. "I, I…"

"Don't argue. We both need to eat."

"I…" How did she say this? "I can't afford to eat at the diner every night." She forced the words out quickly.

He watched her carefully. "What sort of gentleman would I be if I invited a young lady to supper and let her pay?"

Molly couldn't look at him, she felt so embarrassed. He reached out and gently held her chin, forcing her to look at him.

"I'm sorry," she said softly. "I didn't mean to infer anything."

"How many young gentlemen have invited you out then made you pay?" He frowned, obviously annoyed.

She swallowed hard. She didn't want to admit it, but had little choice. "You're the first gentleman to have ever invited me to supper."

His eyes opened wide. "What fools must live in this town!"

She stared up at him, trying to hide her grin, but failed miserably.

"There you go. That's what I like to see." He tightened his grip on her and headed toward the diner. "Tell me about this wishing well. I hear it's supposed to have magical powers." He chuckled as they walked past it.

"I'm sure it does," she said softly. "I feel drawn to it every time there's a full moon."

"What utter nonsense." He stared down at her and grinned.

She stopped walking and stared up at him. "I'm not sure I can dine with someone who ridicules our magical well," she said, forcing a serious look on her face.

He frowned at her. "You're not serious?"

"No, I'm not." She laughed at his reaction, and he joined her.

"Oh, thank goodness for that. You had me for a moment there."

Molly enjoyed strolling through town on the arm of a true gentleman. She could surely get used to it.

* * *

Daniel walked Molly home.

Her little cottage was a short distance outside of Fool's Chance, and he worried about her going there alone. She'd explained she and her aunt always walked home together, so there was no problem, but now...

Now it was downright scary. Walking home alone in the darkness with only the moonlight to guide her terrified Molly each and every night.

He vowed to escort her home each night while he was in Fool's Chance. After that? He didn't want to think about it.

Molly was special. She made his heartrate kick up whenever she was near. Warmth flooded his entire body when he touched her, and he relished it.

"Here we are," she said, digging into her reticule for the key.

He reached over and took it out of her hand, unlocking the door. His skin tingled where he'd touched her. "Molly..." He gazed into her blue eyes. They were bright like sapphires under the moonlight. She stared at him momentarily then tore her eyes away.

"Thank you for a lovely night, Daniel. The meal was wonderful, and I really appreciate you walking me home."

She turned to go inside. He didn't want the night to end.

"I enjoyed your company, Molly. Perhaps we can do it again."

She seemed to contemplate him. "That sounds lovely."

He couldn't help but grin. "Tomorrow night then? I'll pick you up at the store."

She frowned at him. "You can't take me out every night. It's far to expensive."

"I can, and I will." He reached for her hand and caressed it. Her skin was so soft. He enclosed her tiny hand in both of his. "Miss Mason," he said dramatically. "Will you accompany me to supper tomorrow night?"

She couldn't refuse such a request, surely.

He waited patiently as she contemplated his request. "Of course, Mr Emerson." She laughed as she spoke the words.

He loved it when she laughed, which sadly wasn't very often, and he wanted to see more of it.

Molly worked far too hard, and he suspected for far too little. He wanted to help her change that.

"Well, goodnight, Daniel," she said, but he didn't want the night to end. He needed to find a way to detain her longer, to give him more time with her.

"I hear there's a dance at the church hall in a few weeks, Molly. Will you accompany me?"

She stared at him, defiance written all over her face. "I thought you'd be gone by then. You and Eloise."

Why did she think that? He was staying at least until the gown was finished. If he had his way, not even once it was done.

His heart fluttered. "I've decided to make it a mini holiday. I want to see more of this lovely countryside."

"Oh? What about your job? Won't they be upset with you?" She frowned at him. She really had no idea.

He shrugged, giving nothing away. "It's all sorted. I am on extended leave."

"Oh. Goodnight then." She turned to leave, and as much as he wanted her to stay, he knew he had to leave her.

"Goodnight. I'll see you in the morning."

She closed the door, and he stood there for a few minutes, absorbing her fragrance which still lingered. Finally he walked away, relishing seeing her again the next morning.

* * *

Molly had worked every spare moment on the gown for Eloise. It was her best yet, she was certain of it.

Eloise stood rigid as the seamstress pinned the bodice in place. "Are you enjoying your time in Fool's Chance?"

"Not really. I'm finding it rather boring."

She could understand that. There wasn't a lot to do in the little town. Unless you worked or were involved with the ladies auxiliary at the church. Most of the married women here were.

"I'm sorry to hear that," Molly said, adding another pin to the garment. She straightened the material and walked all around Eloise, then nodded. "That looks perfect." She stretched her neck to check her diary. "If you can come back at three, we can do a quick fitting."

Eloise sighed. She was obviously fed up. "I promise there won't be too many more. The initial fitting sessions are tedious, I know. Once we get beyond that, it will all be behind us." She smiled and the other woman smiled back.

A rare occurrence.

The bell tinkled and warmth flooded her. "I think your brother is here."

She closed the fitting room door, giving Eloise privacy. "It's coming along nicely," she said in way of greeting.

She was filled with joy over this creation, but also filled with dread. Once the gown was finished, Daniel would leave Fool's Chance and return to Ellisdale. She'd most likely never see him again.

His face fell. Did he feel the same way?

"I've asked Eloise to come back at three today. It will only be a short session. Thirty minutes at most."

He took a step toward her. "Thank you for everything you're doing for my sister," he said, reaching for her hand. When you're not so busy, I'd like to organise more gowns for her."

She stared down at their intertwined hands. Warmth flooded her and she wanted to pull her hand away. At the same time she didn't.

She knew what was happening – she was falling in love with the man standing before her. Soon he would be gone, and Molly would have to continue her life without him.

Go back to how her life was before. Cold and dreary, with no one to share her time with.

She was filled with dread.

"Are you alright, Molly? You've suddenly gone white."

He seemed very concerned for her, but Molly couldn't allow herself to be drawn in further than she already was. She straightened her back and looked up at him. "I'm fine, thank you for asking."

She turned as the door to the fitting room opened. Daniel dropped her hand.

"Ah, there you are," he said to his sister. "I hear it's coming along splendidly."

"It's beautiful, it truly is." She smiled at Molly, then proceeded to head toward the main door. "I'll see you at three."

There was a skip in her step. Something that wasn't there when they first met. At that time, Eloise had a morbid air about her, but it seemed to have gone. Daniel was right – Eloise had needed this.

It was such a pity it had ruined Molly. Or at least her perception of normal. Daniel Emerson had turned her life upside down.

Chapter Four

Saturday morning rolled around quickly.

It was normally her day off, but Molly had so much to do. She especially wanted to finish the gown for Eloise to wear to the Christmas Gala.

At the same time she didn't. Finishing that gown meant Daniel would leave town. And that was the last thing she wanted. She was enjoying his company far too much.

Molly finished washing her breakfast dishes and was about to put her hair up when there was a knock at the door.

Who on earth could be calling at this hour?

She brushed her hands down her poplin dress, to ensure there were no creases. She opened the door gingerly – it was rare for her to get visitors, especially on a Saturday.

She peeked around the wooden door, and saw Daniel Emerson standing there. She opened the door wider.

"Oh! Good morning," she said, her surprise very evident in her voice.

"Good morning," he said cheerfully, as if it was not unusual for him to call on a unattached woman this early. On a Saturday no less!

He stood there gazing at her. She frowned.

"Did you want something, Daniel?"

"I did indeed. But first let me say how beautiful you look today, Molly." She felt the heat creep up her face, and he laughed. "I love it when you blush. You look so cute." He chuckled, but she couldn't see the funny side.

She looked down at her pale blue gown. "This old thing?"

"Anything looks beautiful on you." He reached out and touched her hair. "This is the first time I've seen you with your hair down. You should wear it down more often."

She ignored his comment. "Was there something you wanted?" She had things to do, and was getting impatient with his games.

"Yes, of course. Forgive me," he said. "I was overwhelmed by your beauty." He looked behind him and indicated a wagon. "I thought we could explore the countryside. My sister feigned illness so she didn't have to tag along."

Molly raised her eyebrows. "You wish me to do this without a chaperone?" *What was he thinking?*

Now it was his turn to frown. "I was thinking it would be nice to spend this sunny, albeit slightly cool, Saturday with you." She looked up at him and took pity. He looked totally deflated at her response. "I even hired a wagon, as you can see."

"Well, in that case, it's perfectly alright," she said rather sarcastically.

He stood in front of her laughing. Not just a chuckle, but a full-blown, in your face laugh. How terribly rude of him!

"I had intended to spend the day working on your sister's gown," she said flatly, then turned around and went inside, leaving him waiting on the doorstep.

"Molly?" he said quietly, still standing there, planted to the spot.

His grin was wide when she came back a few minutes later wearing a coat. Perhaps she was doing the wrong thing, but she'd never know if she didn't take the risk.

He looked disappointed. "You put your hair up." He reached out and removed the pins holding her long brown locks in place. She liked the sensation of his fingers running through her hair. It was nice, and she was mesmerized by his touch.

"That's much better," he said, then led her to the wagon. He held her gently by the waist, lifting her deftly up onto the board.

His touch was warm, comforting, and Molly knew she was gone. She'd never felt such an attachment to any man before. But Daniel was special, and she knew if she wasn't careful, her heart would be shattered into a million pieces when he eventually left Fool's Chance.

And that was likely to be sooner rather than later.

* * *

Daniel stared across at Molly sitting next to him on the wagon.

For a minute there, he was certain he'd be leaving alone. She was a plucky young lady – it was evident not only in the fact she ran a business alone, but most women would not have spoken to him in that manner.

The fact he'd enjoyed it was concerning.

From the moment he'd walked in the door of *A Stitch in Time*, he'd felt a connection with Molly Mason.

He'd come to Fool's Chance to acquire a gown for his sister, not to fall in love.

The sad fact of the matter was he was unable to stay here for an indefinite period of time. His business could not run without him on a long-term basis. Unless...

His head was beginning to hurt thinking about what he would do. The last thing he wanted was to leave Molly behind, for he was certain she wouldn't want to leave this tiny paradise.

"You're frowning. Do you have a headache?"

Her voice startled him out of his thoughts, but it was a welcome interruption.

"A small one, but I am certain the fresh air will help." She nodded but didn't seem convinced.

After a few more minutes she reached over and touched his arm. "Turn right here. This road will take us to Hunter Mountain. You can see Fool's Chance and many of the surrounding towns from the very top." She grinned at him and his heart did a flip. Never before had a woman touched his heart, his very soul, the way Molly Mason did.

Back in Ellisdale, women came from everywhere to secure a date with him. He was fed up with the many gold-diggers back home – those hollow women who wanted nothing of him, but all of his money.

Molly was different. She didn't know his background. Of his wealth. It was a happy situation – she like him for being himself.

They seemed to drive forever when Molly finally touched his arm again. "Turn left here. We're almost there."

After driving through acres of pine trees, they came to a clearing. She was right, you could see for miles from up here.

He stopped the horses and put on the brake, then helped Molly down. Their eyes met as he lifted her off the wagon, and he considered kissing those luscious lips, but he knew Molly wouldn't approve.

He chuckled. That had never stopped him before.

She stared at him. "What's so funny."

He immediately composed himself. "For a moment there, I considered kissing you," he said honestly. "But I didn't think you would approve." He kept his grip on her even after settling her on the ground.

Her eyes opened wide. "You wouldn't dare!" She looked totally offended, and he chuckled again.

"I wanted to, I have to admit." He reached out and ran his thumb across her lips. "You're not that sort of woman, Molly, and I would never put you in a compromising situation."

She stared at him for long moments before answering. "I appreciate that, I really do." She hooked her arm through his and led him closer to the edge of the cliff. "That's Fool's Chance down there in front of us." She pointed to the right. "There are several outlying towns over that way – Canson, Elkswood, and Hunter Valley. Of course that last name comes from Hunter Mountain, where we're standing right now." She grinned at him and it just made him want her more.

But he knew with Molly, rushing was not the way to go. Softly, softly would be his motto in this case. He wanted this woman with all his heart, and wanted to marry her, but knew she would never leave Fool's Chance.

Daniel needed to find a way to win Molly over, while allowing her to stay in her much loved town.

His brain was ticking over… he might just have the solution.

* * *

Molly spread the picnic blanket over the damp ground. Daniel had thought of everything. He also had a basket stacked full of a variety of foods. "This looks amazing. I have no idea how you managed it."

"I have friends in high places," he said, then laughed. "Seriously, I went to the bakery yesterday and ordered a picnic basket for three. But of course, then my sister backed out." He grinned. He didn't seem too upset about that. He pulled out two glasses and a bottle of water, then poured them both a drink.

Molly reached in and pulled out the packaged sandwiches. She pulled off the grease proof wrapping and laid the sandwiches between them. "I didn't think I was hungry, but they look delicious."

She reached over and took a triangle of egg and lettuce sandwich. Daniel took one with meat. She nibbled gently, and he watched her as he chomped into his, then took another.

"You are such a lady," he said, laughing.

She pouted. "And you are such a man." She began to giggle and he joined her. It was so nice to laugh again, to have fun. To spend time with someone you were very fond of.

She finished off three corners of the sandwich then sat quietly.

"What are you thinking?" His voice was soft, but commanding.

"I was thinking about how much I enjoy your company."

He grinned. "And I yours." He swallowed down the last mouthful, then reached for her hand. "What are we going to do about it, Molly?"

Instead of answering she jumped up and spun around, taking in the view. He grabbed her hand. "Molly?"

She stared at him. What could she say? That she was falling in love with him? That she felt hollow, empty, when he wasn't around? That she finally felt like she belonged, and soon he would leave?

She couldn't say any of that, because no matter what, her heart would be broken.

Her eyes began to well with tears, but she fought hard to keep them back. He stared into her face and pulled her close.

His arms crept up her back, and it felt wonderful. Daniel tightened his grip, and she didn't want him to ever let go.

A warm tear slid down her face and she wiped it away. She didn't want Daniel to see how weak she was, or to know how attached she'd become to him.

She felt him staring. "Molly? What's wrong?" He loosened his grip, then held her chin, forcing her to look up at him. "Please tell me what's wrong."

Another tear escaped and he wiped it away with his thumb. "Tell me, Molly. Please?"

"I'm going to miss you when you leave," she said quietly, the wind rushing through her hair. Daniel smoothed it down with his fingers.

He pulled her close to him again. "I feel the same. What are we going to do?"

She stepped out of his embrace, straightened her back and flexed her shoulders. "What we're going to do is get on with our separate lives. We survived before, and I'm sure we will again."

She sounded incredibly brave and sure of herself, but Molly was far from brave, and she felt less confident than she'd ever been.

They didn't stay long after that. Her words had dampened their enthusiasm. She hadn't meant to do it, but her heart was breaking and he deserved the truth.

They stood quietly entwined after her heartbreaking words, until the wind picked up. Then they packed up and drove back the way they'd come.

"Would you like a tree?" Daniel asked suddenly, bringing her out of her thoughts.

"What?" His words were out of the blue. She hadn't thought of getting a tree. Had no way of doing so. Aunt Rose always paid one of the teenage boys in town to cut one down for them, but she hadn't bothered since Aunt Rose had passed on.

"A tree. A Christmas tree." He indicated the hundreds of pine trees surrounding the road they traveled on. "I have an axe, borrowed it from the livery. When I said I was coming up here, it was almost foisted upon me." He grinned.

She loved it when he grinned. He had a dimple either side of his mouth, and they were very endearing.

Still, she shook her head. It wasn't worth the effort. Besides, what did she have to celebrate? The man she was falling in love with was leaving her.

He ignored her and locked the brake then climbed down off the wagon. He came around her side and reached to help her down. "You need cheering up, and I think this will do it."

She screwed her face up at him. "Why did you even bother to ask?" Now she was in more of a huff than she was before.

"I don't think I'll ever work you out. You and every other woman I've ever met." Despite his words, he grinned at her. "Come on, let's go find you a nice little tree."

Molly pulled her coat around herself. It was quite chilly amongst the trees.

Daniel wandered around, keeping her close beside him. "What about this one? It looks good and is a nice size for a cottage like yours."

"It's too big," she said, and moved further ahead. "Ooooh, this one!" she said, shouting over her shoulder at him.

Daniel joined her and agreed, then began to chop it down. He suddenly stopped, tilting his head this way and that. "Do you hear it?"

Molly listened too. "It sounds like water. Oh! There are meant to be streams in the mountains somewhere. Fool's Chance came about because gold was found here."

He looked incredulous. "You didn't know about the streams?"

"I don't come up here often. It's not so easy to do on foot." She grinned at him and he nodded, then headed back to the wagon with the tree.

"Let's go check out the stream. Might as well make the most of the day."

He was right. She needed to get out of her somber mood and make the best of their day together. By her reckoning they probably only had a week or so left. Their time together was far too short.

Daniel grabbed her hand and pulled her toward the stream. The closer they got, the louder the sound of water rushing over the rocks.

When they arrived where the forest met the stream, they both stopped and stared. The scene before them was breathtaking.

He squeezed her hand, then lifted it to his lips. "What an amazing sight."

She felt warm all over, and was momentarily speechless. Not only from the scene before them, but his automatic gesture of kissing her hand.

Why did their time together have to end?

"Come on, let's have a closer look." He was like a child in a candy store.

Then she remembered he was from the city. She'd been like that when she'd first arrived in Fool's Chance, only worse. Not only was a small town new to her, she'd hated it.

Hated the fact she couldn't go to the main street and buy whatever she wanted. Hated she'd had to leave all her friends behind and change schools. But worst of all, her mother had died, and Aunt Rose had tried to take over her mother's role.

At least that's how Molly had seen it, until finally, one day, realization hit her. Aunt Rose was trying to help her adjust to her new life, and that included helping her to grieve the loss of her precious mother.

They reached the edge of the shallow stream and Daniel scooped up a handful of water, then put it to his mouth. "Mmmm, this is good. Try some."

She followed suit. "It *is* good. Do you think there's any gold in there," she asked, giggling.

His eyes opened wide. "Gold, eh? I doubt it. If there was gold up here, surely someone would have found it by now."

"You're probably right."

They sat close together beside the stream. The large boulder was perfectly situated and Daniel pulled her close. "What are we going to do Molly? I can't imagine my life without you."

She turned to look at him, and his eyes pleaded with her.

"You can't leave your business here in Fool's Chance, and I can't abandon mine in Ellisdale." His arm crept up around her back. "It's a horrible situation, no matter how we look at it."

She leaned in and rested against his side. Her heart thudded. They were damned no matter what they did.

Was this really what love was all about? She sure hoped not, because if it was, she didn't want to have anything to do with it.

Chapter Five

When Molly awoke, dread filled her.

Today was the day she handed over Eloise's ball gown, and the day Daniel and his sister left Fool's Chance.

Inside she was sobbing. Outside she had to keep up appearances.

She stared at the writing on the window, cursing the place she loved for introducing her to her soulmate, then wrenching him away just as quickly.

She glanced around at the flurries tumbling down from the sky, and knew it wouldn't be long before the snow was full-blown.

In the weeks since Daniel's arrival, she'd spent time with him every day. They'd been the best days of her life. And now he was leaving.

Her heart was shattered and she'd never be able to repair it.

She unlocked the door and went inside. Eloise would have one last fitting this morning, to ensure it was perfect, and then the pair would leave Fool's Chance forever.

It was all she could do to damp down her emotions.

Molly walked through the store to the backroom, part-filling the kettle and replacing it on the wood stove. She pulled a mug down from the cupboard and went into the fitting room.

She swept as she waited for the water to boil, and cleaned up all the stray pieces of thread. She was about to make a mug of coffee when the bell over the door tinkled.

Molly's heart sank.

This would be the end. Her last moments with Daniel Emerson, the man she'd grown far too fond of.

She pulled herself together and forced a smile onto her face. "Good morning," she said cheerfully. Far more cheerfully than she felt.

Eloise was grinning. Daniel looked grim. "Good morning," he said quietly, sounding as pained as she felt.

"If you pop into the fitting room, we'll do a last minute check, and if all is well, you'll be ready to go." She swallowed down the last words, as they filled her with absolute and utter dread.

"Molly…" Daniel called after her, but she didn't want to get involved in a conversation that would surely end in tears. Her tears.

"Can it wait?" She didn't wait for an answer, and joined Eloise in the fitting room. She went all over the garment, double checking everything was as it should be. She tugged on the ribbon to ensure it was properly secured, and made certain the removable brooch she'd added just below the left shoulder would not fall off.

"It's perfect," she told Eloise, and the younger woman smiled gingerly.

"I can't thank you enough," she said. "I know you're upset about Daniel leaving – he's been incredibly cranky, so I'm certain he doesn't want to leave you either."

She couldn't meet the other woman's eyes. What was she to say? She couldn't think of anything positive, so simply didn't answer.

Eloise frowned at her.

"If you take the gown off, I will place it in a box for you."

Eloise nodded. "I'm sorry if I spoke out of turn, but my brother has been miserable since he knew we'd be leaving."

"I will miss you both," Molly said, swallowing back her growing emotions.

She took the finished gown out to the main shop and pulled a large dress box off one of the shelves. She couldn't bring herself to look at Daniel for fear she might burst into tears.

Out of her peripheral vision she could see he stood stiff and tall, watching her every move. She folded the gown carefully, and handed the box over to Eloise. "Enjoy the Christmas Gala," she said quietly, then began to walk toward the back of the shop.

Every step felt like another step closer to doom.

"Molly, can we talk?" His voice seemed far away, and she continued walking, not daring to acknowledge he'd spoken. When she reached the fitting room she slammed the door, and with her back against it, sobbed her heart out.

* * *

That night was one of the hardest Molly had to endure.

Everywhere she looked reminded her of Daniel. He'd collected her from the store each and every night since he arrived, and took her to supper.

They'd spent hours just sitting either in the town square near the wishing well, or in the hotel foyer. They talked a lot of the time, but mostly they just sat snuggled into each other. Occasionally Eloise joined them, but mostly she made herself scarce.

Daniel was going to take her to the dance next week, but now that he'd left town, it wouldn't happen. She certainly wasn't going alone, it would be like all her Saturday nights before he arrived. Instead she would have supper, spend time knitting or doing needlework, then take herself off to bed.

As she left the store, the moonlight played across the glass window. It was a full moon. Legend had it if you made a wish at the Fool's Chance wishing well on a full moon, your wish would come true.

She knew it wasn't true, despite the rumors that abounded around town. But who was she to dismiss local legend?

Molly made her way to the well, and sat on the edge. Remembering what almost happened last time, she was careful not to get too close.

She looked up to the big bright moon, staring down at her from above.

"I love Daniel so much, I wish he could live in Fool's Chance. I wish we could get married and have a beautiful family."

As she quietly said the words, she felt hot tears slide down her face. Molly knew her wish could never come true, and this time her heart truly shattered. She knew this time it could never be put back together.

* * *

Daniel straightened his tie, buttoned his suit jacket, then donned his thick woolen coat.

He draped the scarf his mother had knitted for him around his neck, then snatched up the bouquet of flowers.

Flurries fluttered down from the sky and landed on his face as he strolled out the door and onto the street. He wondered if his reception would be as chilly as the last time he'd seen Molly.

She was none too happy with him, that was for certain.

He shook the flurries away and hoped the snow held off until at least the end of the night. He had plans and he didn't want them ruined.

It was barely daylight with the sun already beginning its descent. Soon it would be dark, with only the moonlight to guide them.

As he headed toward Molly's cottage, Daniel thought about the future. Their future.

It was clear Molly was fully entrenched in Fool's Chance. The same scenario applied to him, only in his case it was Ellisdale. Would they be able to come to a mutual agreement? He sure hoped so.

When he arrived at the cottage, he straightened his tie once more, and ensured his appearance was as it should be. He needed to make a good impression.

He lifted his hand to knock on the door, but hesitated.

Was he doing the right thing by Molly?

He didn't want to wrench her away from her beloved Fool's Chance, and especially *A Stitch in Time*. On the other hand, she could move her business to Ellisdale where it would thrive.

As his wife she wouldn't need to work, but would she despise him for wanting her to stop doing what she loved?

It was all too hard.

He shook himself. He loved Molly more than life itself – they would find a way to make it work, he was certain they would.

He knocked before he changed his mind again.

The door flew open.

Molly stood in front of him, her eyes wide. She stood glaring at him.

"I'm here to take you to the dance," he said.

"I'm not ready. I was sure you weren't coming." she ground out.

His eyes scanned her from head to toe. She was the most beautiful creature he'd ever laid eyes on. How had he had the good fortune to win this beauty over?

But then he went and spoiled it all.

He pushed the flowers toward her. "No hurry, take your time."

Her mouth curled and it took all his effort to not lean forward and claim her lips. "Don't put your hair up."

She stared at him. She knew he preferred it down, as he'd told her so many times. But convention meant she should wear it up. He wouldn't fight her. Not tonight anyway.

She indicated for him to come in out of the cold. He didn't complain.

Her cottage wasn't small, but it wasn't big either. The sitting room was cozy, with a large fireplace, which was roaring right now.

There were three comfortable chairs scattered about and a low table. A lantern sat in the center of it, but wasn't on. There was more than enough light from the fire.

The pale pink gingham curtains were pulled back to let in the light, but no doubt they'd be pulled closed soon.

Off the sitting room were a number of rooms. One he could see into, and it was clearly a kitchen. He presumed the others were bedrooms and a bathroom.

He began to doze in the comfortable chair, which was almost luxurious after enduring the stagecoach ride back into Fool's Chance.

Eloise didn't accompany him this time. She didn't want to infringe on his time with Molly, she'd said. That was rather unselfish of her.

He sensed Molly standing over him and opened his eyes. She wore the prettiest dress he'd ever seen her wear.

The gown was made of sapphire blue, and matched her eyes perfectly. It had a high-necked bodice and neckline, long sleeves, and had a black panel with buttons from the neckline down to the waist showing off her trim figure.

From the waist down, the layers were ruffled, and there was a contrasting skirt peeking out at the bottom. The long sleeves had a matching embellishment.

Her black boots peaked out slightly below the hem.

Daniel couldn't help but stare.

He shook himself from his sleep-filled stupor, stood, and offered her his arm. They headed for the front door, and were soon on their way.

She didn't say much, apart from small talk, and it was obvious she was still mad at him. He didn't blame her. He had spent every possible moment with her for some weeks, while she made his sister's ball gown, then disappeared.

No wonder she wouldn't speak to him that last day. He wouldn't speak to him either!

Somehow, he had to find a way to make it up to her. He thought the world of Molly – she was very special to him, and he'd hurt her. Unintentionally, but it stung nevertheless.

It was obvious from the pained look on her face he'd made her suffer.

They arrived at the venue, and he handed over their tickets. He looked about, endeavoring to learn the layout of the place, and perhaps get a reading on the way it would be run.

He watched as Molly did the same.

He spotted some empty chairs and accompanied her there. The band were just finishing off a tune, and he urged her to dance to the next one. She was reluctant.

That was fine. They would sit and talk for a while. They did a lot of that when he was in Fool's Chance before, and it had brought them closer. He hoped it would work again. Right now he was not the most popular person in Molly's eyes.

A few more renditions went by, then a call for refreshments. Daniel hooked her arm through his, and took Molly to get refreshments. She didn't refuse but he sensed she was only going through the motions.

She was quiet tonight. Far too quiet for his liking. *Was it too late? Had she lost all confidence in him?*

He certainly hoped not.

The music began again, and the food was cleared away. "Molly, may I have this dance?"

She glanced at him, determination written all over her face. She was going to refuse, he could see the stubbornness to her features.

He leaned in and whispered. "Please, Molly? I've come a long way to escort you here tonight." He straightened up and waited.

She stared up at him, and her face softened.

His relief was palpable.

He reached out for her hands. They were so soft, and were tiny against his. He guided her to the dance floor, then pulled her up against himself, at first keeping a distance between them, but eventually pulling her closer.

Much to his disappointment, Molly didn't relax into him, likely aware of the prying eyes.

He could feel those eyes on them, but didn't care. He did not hide the fact he was in love with one of Fool's Chance's favorites.

They would have to get used to seeing him with Molly. Because by her side was where he belonged.

The music stopped, and instead of leading her back to their seats, he led her outside. It was cooler out there, but more private. And right now, privacy was what he craved.

"Are you enjoying yourself," he asked as he pulled her along behind him. She was obviously reluctant to go outside, alone with him.

"Except for everyone watching us? I am, thank you." She was still annoyed, he could tell. Her words were forced, and there was an undercurrent of anger in them.

"They won't watch us out here. We're close enough it won't cause a problem either, and we can still hear the music."

The tiniest hint of a smile appeared on her lips. If only he could kiss those lips – his longing was relentless, but Daniel knew he couldn't compromise Molly. Especially not for his own selfish needs.

She stood by his side, waiting for the band to start up again. The moment the music began, he pulled her to him. This time she moved in closer, almost snuggling into him. Daniel did not complain.

He held her dainty hand, and felt her other arm slip behind him. He did the same.

Her head rested on his chest, and he was certain she would hear his heart beat a tattoo. It was racing, and there was nothing he could do to stop it.

He liked it out here. On the outskirts of the building they were almost hidden. The doors were opened wide, so it wasn't as though they couldn't be seen, but no one was watching, unlike when they were inside.

Molly relaxed totally into him, and he reveled in the feel of her next to him. He leaned down and whispered so only she could hear. "I love you Molly Mason." Then he lifted her chin to look up to him, and gently kissed her lips.

"I love you too, Daniel," she said. "But it's an impossible situation. We both know that." Tears began to well in her eyes, and he pulled her closer.

He hated to see her upset. He especially hated that he was the cause of it.

"I can't imagine my life without you," he said, then kissed her again. He had to find a way for them to be together, but what that was, he had no idea.

They both had their separate lives, and lived so far apart. There had to be a way, but what that was, he didn't know. Not yet, anyway.

Daniel pulled her closer, determined to make their time together special.

They stayed outside for what seemed an eternity. They were happy there together, alone.

That is until Mrs Grayson stuck her head outside and stared at them. "Molly, my dear," she said firmly. "Why don't you come back inside."

His heart sank. Why couldn't people just leave them alone?

Mrs Grayson moved closer. "People are talking, my dear," she whispered. "We can't have that."

"No we can't," Daniel said gruffly, then escorted Molly back inside where they sat and waited for the night to end. Deep down he knew Mrs Grayson was only trying to help.

They strolled back to Molly's cottage was just as uncomfortable as the on the way to the dance. She barely said a word, and he couldn't blame her. He knew the locals were trying to protect her, but protect her from what? From him?

He was an upstanding man of the community and he would never do anything to discredit Molly's reputation.

But of course they didn't know that. He wasn't from around here - Daniel Emerson was a complete stranger to the people of Fool's Chance.

Perhaps he needed to remedy that.

As they continued to walk, snow began to fall. Not just flurries this time, but snow. Real snow. Cold and heavy. Molly pulled her thick coat around herself, and Daniel seized the opportunity to pull her close. He used the pretense of keeping her warm, but it was much more than that. To him at least.

With his arm tightly wrapped around her, he stared down into her face. Her cheeks were pink from the cold air, and her teeth were chattering. He pulled off his coat and wrapped it around her.

"Oh no, I can't take that," she said. "You'll freeze."

He wrapped it tighter around her. "We're almost there, and your teeth are chattering. We can't have that," he said, stopping to envelope her in an effort to warm her more.

"I appreciate it, Daniel, I really do," she said looking up into his face. "But now you are cold."

"I've been colder," he said, shrugging off her words. "Besides, you have a roaring fire back at the cottage. I'll warm up quickly."

She still didn't look convinced but they carried on walking. She pulled her key out of her reticule as they arrived, and unlocked the door. His hand covered her gloved one, and she stood stock still.

As she stepped inside, she returned his coat. "Thank you for a lovely night," she said, effectively brushing him off.

He was pained. He thought she'd at least invite him inside for a hot cocoa. "Can I at least warm up at the fire?"

"I, uh,"

She looked around, as if checking to see if anyone was watching. He couldn't blame her. Reputation was everything, and these small towns could be relentless to young women if they thought they'd done the wrong thing.

Especially when a man was involved.

He stared down at her, and was about to walk away when she yielded. "I supposed it would be alright," she said quietly, and opened the door wider to let him pass.

He rushed toward the fire, and put out his hands to warm them up. She stared at him, then reached out and held his hands. "Oh my gosh, you're freezing."

As she touched him, a shiver shot up his arm. It wasn't the first time. Whenever Molly touched him, wonderful sensations flooded his body.

He wasn't adverse to them, and reveled in them. "Molly," he said quietly, tightening his grip on her small hands. "What are we going to do, Molly?" he asked, his pain evident in the way his voice cracked.

As she looked up at him, her eyes shone. "I honestly don't know," she said so quietly he almost missed it.

* * *

It was a bitter-sweet day. Their last day together.

Daniel would pick her up and they'd attend church together. For the last time.

She swallowed back the emotion that threatened to overtake her. Instead Molly concentrated on putting her hair up.

Her hands stilled.

Why not leave it down today?

For Daniel.

He preferred it that way, and it was after all, their last day together. Forever.

The thought broke her heart. How could she endure life without her newfound love?

Molly thought she was happy before, but meeting Daniel had changed her life. She'd never be the same again.

She stared at her reflection in the mirror. Who was that unhappy woman staring back at her?

Molly swiped at the trail of moisture on her face. Why did she have to meet Daniel?

The moment the thought entered her head she pushed it aside. She was all the better for having known him, and she didn't regret a moment of their time together.

The knock on the cottage door startled her, and she quickly gave her hair a last brushing, and wiped the tears away.

Molly ran her hands down her dress, despite knowing it was already perfect. She took a deep breath and headed for the door, snatching up her well-worn Bible from the bedside table.

"Good morning."

Daniel had the same sad look she'd seen in her own reflection. "Good morning," she said feeling a little more cheerful now he was standing in front of her.

She was about to close the door when he interrupted her. "Forgotten something?"

She stared at him. What could she have forgotten?

"You'll need a coat," he said, pointing to the snow falling down around them.

Shoving the door open again she grabbed her coat, gloves, and scarf, quickly pulling them on with Daniel assisting her.

He always had her best interest at heart.

They strolled silently toward the little church of Fool's Chance built in 1858 at the peak of the gold rush.

They found seats at the back of the room, endeavoring to be unseen. No such luck.

"Good morning Molly, Mr Emerson." Mrs Grayson gave her a wink and turned back toward the front of the church. The preacher was entering, his bible in his hands.

This week's sermon was all about loving your neighbors and treating others as you want to be treated.

Very timely considering Christmas was fast approaching.

Molly started as she felt Daniel's hand sliding into hers. It surely wasn't appropriate behavior for church, but given they'd soon be separated, Molly didn't complain or brush his hand aside.

It was comforting having her hand in his. She couldn't begin to describe the feeling of knowing he was the one for her.

But not for much longer. She was such an emotional mess she hated to think what she would be like once he was gone.

Banished from her life forever.

Molly couldn't stop the tears filling her eyes, and turned her head to stop him noticing.

She breathed a sigh of relief when the preacher called for everyone to bow their heads in prayer. It would give her a chance to compose herself.

As they filed out of the church and chatted with Preacher Jones, Molly recalled she once thought the preacher may have one day wed them.

All hope of that now dismissed.

Chapter Six

"Of course, Mrs Grayson. I can do that."

Molly led the older woman over to the rolls of plush velvet. She held the soft mauve material up against her long-time customer. "This color suits your eyes perfectly."

"Thank you, Molly. Can I have my usual design, please?"

Molly wished Mrs Grayson would try something different, but at her age, her best customer wasn't willing to change. "Of course, Mrs Grayson. Let me do a quick measure to ensure nothing has changed, and you can be on your way."

They went to the fitting room, and the older lady began to chatter, as she always did. "Did you see they're doing something to the old bank building?" She looked down at Molly who was checking the length.

"No, I didn't. I'm rarely outside during the day, Mrs Grayson." She wrote down the measurement, then checked the waist. "What are they doing there?"

"Well," Mrs Grayson said, quite animated now. "It appears they're renovating the inside. Modernizing it perhaps."

"It would be nice if we had a real bank here instead of just the Mercantile, don't you think?" Molly always worried her money wasn't safe at the Mercantile.

"Oh, that it would be, Molly. But I can't imagine it. Can you?"

"Hold out your arm please, Mrs Grayson." Molly held the tape measure to the older woman's shoulder.

"No, I can't, my dear. And my Henry, God rest his soul, always said Fool's Chance was far too small to have its own bank. I can't imagine that's changed."

Molly nodded. She needed to concentrate on what she was doing. "All done. I can have it ready by...." She glanced across at her diary. "Next Wednesday – if that works for you?"

"Perfect. Thank you, Molly." Mrs Grayson moved in and hugged Molly. The other woman was almost a mother figure to her since Aunt Rose had passed on.

"It's a pity that Daniel had to leave," she said. "He would have made a perfect husband for you, Molly."

"Yes, he would have," she said much quieter than she'd intended. "Wednesday then." She guided her customer out the door before the flood gates opened. It had been less than a week since Daniel left, and Christmas wasn't far away. She was trying to push him to the back of her mind so she could at least enjoy the Christmas festivities.

She went outside and glanced down the street. They were indeed doing something to the bank. She had no bookings for another fifteen minutes, so she strolled down to check it out.

The workmen were busy inside, building and changing things around, as Mrs Grayson had reported. It peaked her interested. *What on earth was going on there?*

Molly shrugged her shoulders. She'd find out soon enough.

As she glanced back toward *A Stitch in Time*, she saw her next customer had arrived early. She pushed the old bank building to the back of her mind, and rushed back to her little shop.

* * *

Molly closed up early.

She had no more customers booked in for the day, and tiredness had set in. Tomorrow she would close the store for the day and do an inventory. It would not do to run out of fabric.

Most of her suppliers closed over the holiday period, and she couldn't afford to lose business due to no supplies to work with.

She was too tired to cook tonight, but she didn't feel like going to the diner, and instead called into the Sugar and Spice Bakery.

"Good afternoon, Molly."

"Hello Mrs Hardy. Do you have any Cornish pasties left?" She looked around at the decorated store. She hadn't bothered with decorating *A Stitch in Time*. Especially when she'd been feeling so low.

Mrs Hardy reached into the glass display case and placed the item in a paper bag. "I have one apple slice left here – with my compliments."

"Thank you, Mrs Hardy. That's so lovely of you."

Molly handed over payment and the other woman came around to the other side of the counter. "I heard about your Mr Emerson. Such a pity," she said.

She reached for Molly's hand and patted it. "You'll see – another young man will come along and steal your heart."

She thanked the bakery owner and walked out. She didn't want anyone else – she wanted Daniel. Why couldn't people understand that?

Molly passed the old bank as she headed for home. It was still daylight, which was quite a change for her. Workmen were in the process of adding a sign to the side of the old bank. "Fool's Chance Bank" it read in big black letters.

She glanced across and saw a notice on the glass doors indicating the new bank would open the following Friday.

That meant it would open before Christmas. She wondered what the owners of Casey's Mercantile thought of that, since they would no longer have the bank agency.

She shrugged.

It suited her fine. She'd always worried her money wasn't safe at the Mercantile's branch of the Ellisdale bank.

She stared through the glass doors into the interior of the building. It was still quite a mess, but a handful of workers were diligently working on it.

For a moment, she wondered who owned it, but decided she didn't really care. So long as her money was safe, she had no interest.

* * *

Friday seem to come around more quickly than Molly thought it would.

Not that she was complaining. She'd decided to take advantage of the new bank opening today.

She closed the shop while she collected up the week's takings, then went to the bank to open an account.

She was relieved Fool's Chance finally had a real bank. It would be much more secure than the Mercantile, which had already been robbed once. Not recently, but at the peak of the gold rush.

She stared up at the large sign on the outside – Fool's Chance Bank. It had a nice ring to it.

She peered in the door. Despite the town being small, it was quite busy. She recognized some customers as being from outlying towns.

Fool's Chance was far closer than Ellisdale, and the bank might bring other business to town.

It was a shining light on an otherwise bleak time.

Daniel was never far from her mind. The memory of him was everywhere – in the little store where they first met, his memory was particularly high.

She would sometimes look up from her sewing machine and imagine him standing there, watching her. She smiled at the thought.

What she would give to have him here with her again.

Her heart raced and she put her hands to her chest. Molly closed her eyes and his image drifted into her mind.

"It's quite exciting isn't it?" Mrs Grayson brought her out of her thoughts.

She put on her best smile and turned toward the older lady "It really is," Molly said, finding it difficult to get excited about anything lately .

She made her way to the next available teller and opened her bag of money. "I'd like to open an account and make a deposit," she said.

"Please complete this form," the teller said, pushing the form toward her.

Once she had completed all the fields the teller quirked an eyebrow at her. "Thank you, Miss Mason. Please take a seat. The bank manager is interviewing all business owners who open an account."

"What about my money?"

" I can process that while you wait."

He counted the takings and supplied a receipt, then indicated for her to sit. Then the teller disappeared from sight.

When he reappeared it was to get her to follow him to the manager's office.

She'd only planned on being away from the store 15 minutes at most, and this was becoming a distraction she didn't count on.

Molly was shown to a pretty reception area where she had to wait .

She'd not long sat, when a familiar voice spoke her name. "Molly."

Her head spun around and she stumbled to her feet. "Daniel?" Her heart thudded. Surely she was dreaming.

He stepped forward and enveloped her, pulling her close as though she was his lifeline. "I've missed you more than you'll ever know," he said close to her ear.

There was so much she wanted to say, but she'd been struck dumb.

Her mouth wasn't connecting with her brain. Instead her arms went up and around him and held on for dear life.

Was this really happening? She was certain she'd never be held by the love of her life again.

He said he'd find away and she should have believed him.

"How…?"

His lips interrupted her question, but she wasn't complaining.

It was good to be back in his arms.

* * *

Daniel melted into Molly's arms.

It was only days since he'd left her, since his heart had been shattered, but it felt like a lifetime.

It hadn't been easy pulling this altogether, but he'd managed it.

His stress levels were high worrying it couldn't be done in time for Christmas. Somehow they'd pulled it off.

He'd prayed to spend Christmas with Molly – nothing was more important to him. He had a good team of construction workers. Without them, none of this would be possible.

He had been keeping secrets from her, and as far as he could tell, she still hadn't worked it out.

Right now at this very moment, he didn't care. All that mattered was that Molly was back in his arms where she belonged.

He pulled her closer.

How he managed to keep his return to Fool's Chance a secret, Daniel still didn't know. In a town this size it was almost impossible.

"I have to go," she said quietly. " I have a booking."

"Cancel it," he said, tugging her closer still.

She shoved out of his arms. "I can't do that," she said indignantly. "You of all people should understand."

She was right. It was unprofessional and downright rude. He should never have suggested it.

He looked down into her face. She was disappointed with him.

"I'm sorry," he said, genuinely apologetic "I'm being selfish of course."

Her face softened. *Did that mean she forgave him?* "Dinner?"

She seemed wary.

They'd been down this path before. He would ask her to dinner, and they'd have a great night. Then he'd leave.

Only this time he wasn't leaving. Fool's Chance was now his forever home.

Provided Molly agreed to be his wife. If not there is no future for him here.

Chapter Seven

Molly was ecstatic as she returned to *A Stitch in Time*.

Daniel was back.

Daniel was back!

She could barely fit her key into the lock, she was so excited.

Her heart was racing, and her whole body shook. Never in her wildest dreams did she think she'd ever see Daniel Emerson again.

She went out to the back room and sat down, trying to get her wits about her. Trying to calm her heart rate, calm herself.

Her next customer was due to arrive in a matter of minutes, and she needed to be in control of her emotions.

She took several deep breaths. It did help, but she was still shaking.

As the bell over the door tinkled, she had a thought. *What if Daniel left again?*

She gasped. After all she'd been through already, she couldn't cope with that. Daniel had invited her to dinner, but now she wondered if she should even go.

She slapped her hands to her forehead. Her head was spinning with scenarios, and her heart thudded in her chest.

Molly was devasted.

At first she was elated at his return, but what if this wasn't permanent? How would she cope with that?

She shook her head trying to chase the negative thoughts away.

"Hellooooo."

Mary Dimple was here, and waiting for her appointment. She stood, straightened her back and stretched her shoulders, then stormed out into the shop where one of her best customers stood waiting for her fitting.

"I'm sorry to have kept you waiting, Mrs Dimple," Molly said apologetically. "This will be your final fitting, unless we need to make adjustments."

She led the customer into the fitting room, and tried to concentrate on the job at hand. Unfortunately, Daniel was constantly at the back of her mind.

* * *

Daniel stood in the near-darkness looking down into the wishing well.

"I'm told you have magical powers," he said into the moonlit water. "I desperately need your help."

He had sensed Molly was reluctant. That she thought he may not stay this time. She couldn't be further from the truth.

"I need your magic. Help me convince Molly to marry me."

His voice caught in his throat as he said the words. *What would he do if Molly turned him down?*

He shook his head. He couldn't afford to think like that.

Daniel looked up as he heard a door close. It was Molly locking up. He sprinted toward her but stopped in his tracks when she glared at him.

He swallowed hard.

Was she having second thoughts about him? His heart thudded. "Molly, I..." She gazed at him. "We're going to dinner, right?"

She shrugged.

"I mean, we made that arrangement?" They did, didn't they? Right there in the bank, while he held her in his arms.

He wanted to hold her again. He stepped forward.

As his arms enveloped her, she backed off. He stared down into her face. "Molly?" Confusion overtook him.

Was she angry at him for going away?

But he came back. He came back for her. He couldn't bear to be away from her – his heart was broken without her. Shattered.

He felt hollow and barely survived without her.

She began to walk away. Slowly at first, but then she picked up pace. He caught up quickly, and grabbed her arm in an effort to make her look at him, talk to him.

"What's going on, Molly?"

She rounded on him. "How do I know you won't leave again?" She spat the words at him, and he could hear the pain in her voice, see the agony etched in her features.

He reached out for her, but she pushed him away. "I can't do this again, Daniel. It's like a game of cat and mouse. You say you love me, but then you leave. You come back, and you leave again."

She closed her eyes tight and he knew she was fighting back her emotions. Suddenly she opened her eyes and stared at him. "How do I know you won't leave me again?"

He glanced at her, then at the wishing well. He'd made his wish, his pleading wish, but would it be enough? "I won't leave again, Molly. I want to be here with you."

She shook her head as though she was shaking off his words.

"Can we at least go somewhere and eat? You must be hungry, and I know I am."

She stood with her hands on her hips – she was really annoyed with him. He worried that he'd left it too late to tell her how he really felt.

He watched as her tongue darted out and licked her lips. It took all his willpower not to pull her into his arms and kiss her. But he knew he was already on shaky ground.

"I am hungry," she said quietly.

He mentally celebrated, but couldn't risk being seen outwardly rejoicing. She might change her mind again.

The snow was heavier now. The closer to Christmas it got, the heavier the snowfall. Molly pulled her coat tighter around herself, and wrapped her scarf around her neck. He took the opportunity to move closer.

"Are you cold? Let me help." He pulled her tighter against him and put his arm around her shoulder. It was certainly no burden. In fact he was enjoying it.

He'd expected her to push him away, but she didn't. Instead she looked up at him, and stared into his eyes.

"You've got snow in your hair," she said, giggling. She reached up and brushed it away, and her glove-covered fingers brushed against his forehead.

It may not have been her bare skin, but the contact still sent a shiver down his spine.

He reached up and imprisoned her hand. "Molly," he said quietly, bringing her hand to his lips. "I've missed you enormously."

He watched as she swallowed, her sapphire eyes studying him. "I've missed you too," she said softly, as though the admission was a difficult one.

Daniel was engulfed by emotion, and could barely speak. Instead he brushed stray hair back behind her ears.

She continued to study him. It was unnerving.

He couldn't fathom what she was thinking. He dreaded to think.

Without warning, she got up on her tippy-toes and kissed him gently on the lips, then looped her arm through his. "I guess if we're going to dinner, we'd better make a move."

Her lips turned up slightly, as though she wasn't certain if she should smile or not. But Daniel had no such reservation and grinned broadly.

He couldn't help himself.

* * *

"I thought we'd be going to the diner," Molly said as they entered the Royal Hotel.

"The hotel dining room is a little quieter. It will be easier to talk here." Daniel put his hand over hers. "You don't mind do you?"

Did she? She didn't think so. They'd been to the diner so many times now, it was becoming difficult to find something on the menu she hadn't had before.

"Not at all." She smiled at him tentatively. She was still quite concerned he might disappear on her again. But as Manager of the bank, perhaps that would entice him to stay.

They were greeted at the dining room door by a hostess, who guided them to their table. Molly had never been in the Royal Hotel's dining room before. In fact, she'd never been in the hotel.

It was kind of fancy. Okay, it was a lot fancy. Far superior to anything she'd seen before.

It was mostly business people that went there, as well as rich travelers who stopped on their way to some place more suitable for tourists. Like Ellisdale.

She mentally screwed up her nose. She didn't like big cities – she preferred the peace and tranquility of Fool's Chance.

She looked around. It was lovely. More than lovely – it was quite beautiful. She wondered what the food would be like, but was certain the quality of the food would match the décor.

As though reading her mind, Daniel interrupted her thoughts. "Stunning, isn't it? And the food is amazing." A waitress walked over and handed them each a menu, as if on cue. He continued to speak once she'd left them alone. "I did some research, and the hotel was built at the height of the gold rush. The original owners made a fortune from it, and retired on the profits."

She quirked an eye at him. She didn't realize he was into history. "You surprise me," she said. "You know more about Fool's Chance than I do. I feel quite ashamed."

"Don't be. When the decision was made to re-open the bank here, I did some checking."

She stared into his face. "Did they force you to come?" She needed to know if he was here voluntarily or not.

He reached across the table and covered her hands with his. "The bank was re-opened because I wanted to come here. To be with you."

Should she believe him? On the other hand, why shouldn't she?

Her heart skipped a beat. *Did his boss really open the bank here in Fool's Chance so he could be here with her? What sort of boss does that?*

She didn't share her thoughts in case he somehow felt affronted. Instead she smiled. She felt a little more relaxed now.

"How did your booking go this afternoon?"

She snatched up one of the menus and pretended to be studying it. "It went well. It was the last fitting for Mrs Dimple. Finally. That woman keeps losing weight. I've had to alter the garment at least five times. And it's not even finished yet!"

She knew she must look exasperated, because that's how she felt. She glanced up to see Daniel laughing. "What's so darned funny?" Now she was feeling annoyed.

He immediately made his face blank. "How dare she lose weight. The cheek of the woman!"

He was so straight-faced that Molly suddenly burst into laughter. He was right. As if it was a major issue.

"Are you ready to order?" Molly startled. The waitress seemed to come out of nowhere.

"Sorry, we've been chatting. Give us a few more minutes would you?"

"Of course, Mr Emerson."

She hurried away, and Molly stared down at the menu. "What do you recommend?" At his own confession, Daniel had eaten here before, so perhaps he had some favorites.

He glanced across at her and grinned. "Everything. The food is amazing. Tastes like home-cooked, only better."

"Better because you don't have to wash the dishes, better?" That was always the added benefit to eating out. At least in Molly's mind.

"There is that about it." He picked up the menu again. "The lamb shanks in gravy are mouth-watering. Melt in your mouth, in fact. Served with mash and carrots." He went back to the menu. "The steak with fried potatoes is good too. Or there's the…"

She interrupted him. "The lamb shanks sound good." Molly dropped her menu on the table and stared at him. "I honestly didn't take you for a lamb shank kind of man." She grinned. She learned something new about him every time they were together.

Daniel signaled for the waitress, and she scurried back. She took their orders and quickly departed again, returning a short time later with a plate of bread and two glasses of water.

It didn't seem much longer and their meal was placed in front of them. Molly leaned down and breathed in the aroma of her food.

"Smells delicious." She'd never been so enticed by food before. Aunt Rose had been a terrific cook, but it never smelled as good as this.

He grinned at her. "Dig in."

That's exactly what she did. Molly was in food heaven. She knew she was hungry, but didn't realize how totally famished she was – she finished every scrap on her plate.

"You've got…" Daniel waved in the direction of her lips.

She frowned. "I've got what?"

He leaned in. "You have a tiny bit of gravy in the corner of your mouth. She reached for the linen napkin, but he beat her. A gentle finger swiped at the gravy, then his finger went to his mouth.

"Mmmmm."

"Hey! You stole my dinner!"

They both broke out in laughter. Molly felt at least a dozen eyes staring at them, and she looked about. She didn't recognize anyone in the dining room. Not that she expected too – the dining room was reserved for guests.

The waitress cleared away their empty plates, and returned with coffee. "Would you like the dessert menu, Mr Emerson?

"Yes please." He stared at Molly, as though daring her to say no.

Why not indulge this one night?

At her request, Daniel ordered for them both. Steamed Orange Pudding with clotted cream. It sounded delicious. And it was.

Soon after their dishes had been cleared away, Molly was ready to leave. "I have an early start again tomorrow," she said, regret evident in her voice.

He reached out and covered her hand with his. "Just a few more minutes? Then I'll walk you home."

She nodded but also protested. "I am quite capable of walking myself home. It's not very far."

"Not on my watch, Molly. I need to ensure you get home safely." He leaned in and kissed her cheek. "I couldn't live with myself if anything happened to you."

She was about to protest again when he put his fingers to her lips. She fought back the emotion that rose to the surface. He really did care about her.

As she stared into his face, he signaled to the waitress.

Three men strolled over to their table, and stood in a half circle. Before she knew what was happening, they began to play their violins.

Daniel had hired violinists to play to them?

Soon after the music began, he dropped to his knees beside her. "Molly," he said, his eyes glistening. "Will you marry me?"

He held an enormous diamond ring out to her, and waited. He was stiff, and she could see he was anxious for her response.

"I, I don't know what to say, Daniel." Her heart was beating so hard she thought she might faint right there on the chair.

The room went silent except for the violins playing in the background.

"Just say yes."

Her hands went to her chest. This was what she wanted, wasn't it? *Why did she hesitate?*

She stared down into his face, but couldn't get the words out.

As if he realized her dilemma, he reached out for her hand and held it. He gave her the courage to make her decision.

"Yes!" Tears streamed down her face, and Daniel grinned broadly.

The dining room erupted into applause.

Chapter Eight

Molly couldn't help but stare at the ring on her finger.

She'd never seen such a massive diamond. Of course she'd protested at the size of it, and at the price he must have paid.

Daniel laughed. She wasn't impressed.

As he walked her home in the moonlight, he explained he didn't work for the bank, but was the bank's owner.

His father was President of the Bank of Ellisdale, and had been training Daniel for the job since he left school.

When his parents died unexpectedly, Daniel was able to seamlessly slip into the position, ensuring the bank continued to prosper, and that no staff lost their jobs.

Now he'd opened a branch in Fool's Chance, he had tellers who would train up some of the local youth to take up those positions here.

It was all so overwhelming. Not only had Daniel asked her to marry him, but in the same evening she found out he was rich?

She must be dreaming. This couldn't possibly be happening. Not to her. Not to little Molly Mason who struggled to stay afloat from week to week.

"A penny for your thoughts."

His voice brought her out of her revelry. "I was trying to process everything that's happened tonight," she said honestly.

She glanced at him to see Daniel nodding. "I know it's hard, and I'm sorry I kept so much from you."

"Why did you?" She rounded on him.

He didn't hesitate. "Because I've had dozens of gold-diggers trying to get me to marry them since my parents died. "But you were different. Are different. You're interested in me for me, not for my money."

He held her by the shoulders and studied her. "I love you, Molly. You are very special to me." He leaned in and kissed her gently on the lips. Her lips tingled where his had been just moments ago.

"I love you too, Daniel," she said quietly. "I know you're not interested in me for my money either."

He grinned at her, then kissed her again.

Daniel held her for the longest time before leaving her. She wished he could stay, but that simply wouldn't be acceptable. The sooner they married the better, but a wedding date wasn't something they'd discussed yet.

* * *

Today was the raising of the Christmas tree in the town center.

It was to be placed not far from the magical wishing well. Whether or not that well had helped him get Molly, he'd never know. One thing Daniel did know, he was unquestionably grateful he'd been advised to bring his sister here to have her gown made.

In his eyes, she'd been the Belle of the Ball. The gown Molly made for Eloise had stood out above every other gown there. She'd even met a young man, a very suitable beau, all because she'd attended the Christmas Gala.

He was so happy for her.

The town's women folk stood around and watched as the men put the tree upright. Now he was engaged to Molly and was staying in Fool's Chance forever, he figured he was one of the locals.

He stepped forward to help. Out of the corner of his eyes, Daniel saw Molly gasp. *Did she think he wouldn't volunteer?*

He was one of them now. He would do whatever was needed.

Daniel held tight to the enormous tree while some of the other men put a rope around it and tied it securely. It would cause a lot of damage if it came down, and this was the safest way.

Once they were done, the children came forward and began to decorate it. The box of decorations was overflowing, and he could see many of them were well-worn.

He could easily replace them with new ones, but Molly had explained they held sentimental value more than anything.

Many of the decorations had been supplied by town folk who had now passed on. To continue using them was to honor their existence.

He wondered if that would happen with decorations they supplied? Molly was already talking about the contribution they would make next Christmas.

After all, she'd said, it was traditional for couples to donate a handmade decoration for their first Christmas together in Fool's Chance.

He liked the thought of that, and it got him thinking.

Not that he would tell Molly. Not yet anyway.

She was busy chatting to Mrs Grayson and Mrs Hardy, so he was able to slip away unnoticed.

* * *

Mrs Grayson lifted Molly's hand and stared at her engagement ring.

"You've done well for yourself, young Molly. I told you he was a good man."

Molly grinned. She had, hadn't she?

She watched as the children decorated the tree. Christmas was, after all, more about the children than adults.

She looked around, but couldn't see Daniel. Where had he gone?

She saw him talking to someone, but the tree branches blocked her view, and without being obvious, she couldn't see who.

The raising of the Christmas tree was a big deal in Fool's Chance. Everyone joined in. All the businesses that would normally be open, closed for the raising, then reopened afterwards.

Things had slowed down for Molly, now the festivities had taken over, so she wasn't overly concerned.

"You'll have to start working on your wedding arrangements," Mrs Grayson said, pulling Molly close and hugging her. "I'm so excited for you." She squeezed Molly a little tighter.

Wedding arrangements? There wouldn't be much to arrange.

If only Aunt Rose was here now. Her father also wasn't here to walk her down the aisle.

A tear trickled down her face at the thought. It was meant to be a happy time, but she suddenly felt sad.

"What's this then," Mrs Grayson asked.

"I was thinking about dear Aunt Rose and my parents," she said quietly, swiping at her errant tears. She pulled out of the older woman's arms and began to walk away from the crowded tree. "It won't be a big wedding anyway," she said. "It will be a quiet affair. Just Daniel and me, and the required witnesses."

She glanced at Mrs Grayson and Mrs Hardy who were both staring at her in horror. "What do you mean? Of course you're having a big wedding!"

Molly shook her head. "I'm sure Daniel won't want that."

"You haven't discussed it?" Mrs Grayson was determined if nothing else.

"No. No we haven't." She looked from one woman to the other. She knew they meant well, but in this instance, they wouldn't get their way. Molly was certain Daniel wouldn't be interested in a big wedding. He was just like her – he liked to keep private things private.

Mrs Hardy looked about. "Where is that handsome young man of yours anyway?"

Molly glanced about. "I honestly don't know. I saw him talking to someone earlier, but couldn't see who it was." She shrugged. "I'm sure he'll find me if he wants to."

She turned and strolled toward *A Stitch in Time*. The fitting room needed a tidy, and while it was quiet was a perfect time to do it.

* * *

Molly's eyes fluttered open.

Today was the day – the day she would marry Daniel.

Her heart pounded. Could it really be true?

She sat up in bed, sliding her legs onto the floor. It was like a dream come true. One she never believed would come to fruition.

Flipping through the gowns in her robe, Molly pulled out her favorite. It was a modest style, with a high neckline, and was made from a pretty floral material. Aunt Rose helped her make this one, and it had always been a favorite.

Molly had long dreamed of a big wedding, but it wasn't to be. As long as she was with her soulmate, nothing else mattered.

She proceeded to the bathroom and stared at her reflection in the mirror. Her hair was a mess. She was a mess.

Using the ornate pitcher Aunt Rose had received as a wedding gift all those years ago, Molly filled the matching porcelain bowl with water and proceeded to wash herself all over.

She had prepared some rose water a few days beforehand, and would later adorn herself with that. She hoped the floral fragrance would fill Daniel with happiness.

She brushed her hair, leaving it down. When she was done, she pulled her robe around herself.

Molly was too excited to eat, and instead poured herself a cup of tea.

Daniel would be here to collect her soon. They would go to the church together, and Preacher Jones would marry them.

She put her hands to her chest. Was this really happening? She certainly hoped so.

It was a pity Aunt Rose wasn't here to see it. She would have loved Daniel. If it wasn't for *A Stitch in Time*, they would never have met – that was blatantly obvious.

Tears threatened, but Molly forced them back. Today was meant to be happy, not a day for reflecting on what might have been.

She pulled on her gown and boots, then checked herself in the full-length mirror. Everything seemed perfect. Her gown was perfect, her hair was perfect. Now all she needed was a perfect wedding with her perfect man.

She reached for her best shawl at almost the same time there was a knock on the door. Daniel was early!

Molly took some deep calming breaths. She didn't want to appear panicked. Not on her wedding day.

She slowly opened the door. Daniel stood before her resplendent in his best suit. She couldn't help but grin.

He leaned in and kissed her gently on the lips, reaching for her hands at the same time. "Good morning," he said, pulling her in for a hug.

"Oooh, don't crush my dress," she admonished him, then wanted to take back her words. She glanced up at him. "I, I'm sorry. I want to look my best for the ceremony."

"Of course you do." He looked her up and down, then grinned. "You look positively stunning, Molly. I can't believe some young man hasn't snapped you up before this."

She couldn't help but smile.

"But I'm so glad they didn't." He moved closer, then kissed her forehead.

Molly snatched up her reticule, then changed her mind and decided to leave it behind. It was a simple ceremony – she really didn't need it.

"Are you sure you won't need it?" Daniel asked.

She shrugged her shoulders and snatched it up again. It gave her somewhere to put her house key, so why not. Her kerchief was in there too.

Soon they were on their way, and Molly's heart fluttered more than once as they approached the church. As they stood outside, she was sure she could hear voices.

She shook her head. That couldn't be right. It was just her and Daniel, the preacher and their two witnesses.

Daniel opened the heavy doors and stood aside for her to enter. Molly couldn't believe her eyes – nearly everyone from Fool's Chance was in that little church. They'd come to celebrate her marriage to Daniel.

She couldn't stop her bottom lip from quivering.

"Oh no," Daniel said. "You can't cry on your wedding day." He gently pulled her to him. "I wanted to surprise you."

She looked up into his chocolate brown eyes. Would she ever cease to be surprised by his thoughtfulness?

"Thank you," she said softly, pulling herself together. "That was so lovely of you."

"Anything for you, Molly."

He hooked her arm through his, and they began to walk down the aisle, all her friends nodding and watching as they did. Molly noticed many of her regular customers were there too.

That was just too sweet for words.

Daniel's sister Eloise sat in the front row, along with Mrs Grayson, and Mrs Hardy, who were to be their witnesses.

As they approached Preacher Jones, Mrs Grayson reached out and took her reticule, then hugged Molly tight. Tears were in her eyes, and Molly hoped it wasn't contagious. She didn't want to be red-eyed for her wedding.

"I'm so very happy for you, Molly. You deserve to be truly happy." She glanced at Daniel. "And you – I've got my eye on you, young man." She grinned at him then sat down.

"Dearly Beloved," the preacher began.

It was all too overwhelming, and most of the ceremony was a blur. Molly did remember Daniel kissing her at the end, then leading her into the church hall for the wedding feast her dear friends had prepared.

Epilogue

"No, no, no!" Molly screeched. "I have to finish hemming Mrs Grayson's dress first."

Daniel came to stand beside her. "Molly?" He stared down at her, sitting at the sewing machine in her little store.

She insisted she continue working until her time came, so Daniel insisted on accompanying her.

"Come on, let's get the doc." Daniel was frustrated by his wife's loyalty to her customers, but her welfare had to come first. "We both know dear Mrs Grayson won't be annoyed. She'll be happy our little bundle of joy has finally arrived."

Molly's hands went to her stomach, and her eyes opened wide. "Grab up the dress, Daniel. Quickly," she screamed, then stood.

Daniel stared down at the puddle on the floor. "Well that's it then," he said, holding the dress up so it wasn't spoiled.

Molly sat back down and cried. "I wanted to finish the dress first," she said, her bottom lip quivering.

He gently laid the dress across the table where it wouldn't be damaged, then picked Molly up and strode out the door, closing it behind them.

He summoned the doctor on his way to their little cottage not far away. As much as he insisted on building a mansion for Molly, she insisted on living in the little cottage where she'd lived with her Aunt Rose.

He had to admit it was a cozy place, and suited them perfectly. He'd never been one for all the bells and whistles that came with a rich lifestyle, but as a child he had no choice – he'd had to endure it with his parents.

Besides, as Molly had often told him, a mansion didn't fit with the lovely town of Fool's Chance.

As he unlocked the front door, the warmth of the fire met them at the door. So did the aroma of stew cooking on the wood stove. Molly had insisted on putting it on this morning before leaving for *A Stitch in Time.*

He couldn't believe his good fortune in coming here to arrange a gown for his sister. For Eloise, he would do anything.

As it turned out, fate was on his side.

Daniel looked down at the love of his life, her protruding belly the most beautiful thing he'd ever seen. Apart from her that was. He leaned in and kissed her lips. "I love you Molly Emerson."

He fought back the emotion that still overtook him every time he looked at his wife. Every time he lay in bed with her, and whenever he felt the new life move inside her.

As he gently placed her on the bed, the doctor arrived. He was followed by Mrs Grayson and Mrs Hardy.

Molly's bottom lip quivered again. "I didn't get your gown finished, Mrs Grayson," she said sadly.

"My dear girl! Don't you worry about that. The dress was a distraction, to keep you busy and stop you worrying."

Why was he not surprised? The dear old thing was like a mother to Molly, and now she'd be like a grandmother to their baby.

"Right Daniel. Out." She shoo'd him out of the house like an annoying chicken.

"But…"

"No but's. This is women's business. Not for men. Go on, get." She shoved him out of the room and closed the door in his face.

She quickly opened it again. "Put water on the stove. Lots of it. Big pots full. Tell me when it's boiled."

He nodded and scurried off to do what he was told. It seemed like forever until the water boiled. Molly's screams were unnerving, but if she had to endure it, so did he.

Daniel knocked quietly on the door once the water was ready.

"Ah, Daniel," the doc said. "Right on time. Come and welcome your new son."

"I have a boy?" Daniel's eyes filled with tears, and he didn't care who saw them. He had a son. "What about Molly? Is she alright?"

The doc pulled the door wide open. "Come and see for yourself. She's sitting up, holding the baby."

And sure enough she was. Molly looked across to him, tears filled her eyes too. They had a baby. Together.

The first of many, he hoped. But if it wasn't to be, that was fine too.

They had their little family. And they had their enduring love for each other.

Everything was right in his world.

The End

From the Author

Thank you so much for reading my book – I hope you enjoyed it.

I would greatly appreciate you leaving a review where you purchased, even if it is only a one-liner. It helps to have my books more visible!

About the Author

Multi-published, award-winning and bestselling author Cheryl Wright, former secretary, debt collector, account manager, writing coach, and shopping tour hostess, loves reading.

She writes both historical and contemporary western romance, as well as romantic suspense.

She lives in Melbourne, Australia, and is married with two adult children and has six grandchildren. When she's not writing, she can be found in her craft room making greeting cards.

Links:

Website: *http://www.cheryl-wright.com/*

Blog: *http://romance-authors.com/*

Facebook Reader Group:
https://www.facebook.com/groups/cherylwrightauthor/

Join My Newsletter:
https://cheryl-wright.com/newsletter/